FEAR NO EVIL

ALLEN BROKKEN

Unit Study

CONTENTS

ALLEN BROKKEN

Allen Brokken is a teacher at heart, a husband and father most of all. He's a joyful writer by the abundant grace of God. He began writing the Towers of Light series for his own children to help him illustrate the deep truths of the Bible in an engaging and age-appropriate way. He's dedicated fifteen years of his life to volunteer roles in children's ministry and youth development.

Now that his own children are off to college, he's sharing his life experiences on social media @allenbrokkenauthor and through his blog https://allenbrokkenauthor.com/blog.

INTRODUCTION

Dear Reader,

When my children were middle-grade readers, I had a tough time finding adventure stories they could enjoy that also emphasized Biblical truths. So I began telling them a story about life on the frontier, weaving in points of the faith that I felt they should learn. As the story developed, a unique world of pets with fantastic powers and holy weapons emerged to help the young characters hold back the forces of darkness.

The *Fear No Evil: A Unit Study for Homeschoolers* is a supplement to those tales of adventure. It digs deeper into the spiritual aspects of the story from a Christian perspective. Over the next four weeks, your students will study passages from the story to highlight lessons from scripture and their real life application. There are also activity pages and memory verses to help them internalize the key messages in *Fear No Evil*.

I hope you enjoy the story as much as my own children did.

May God bless you richly,

Allen Brokken

FEAR NO EVIL

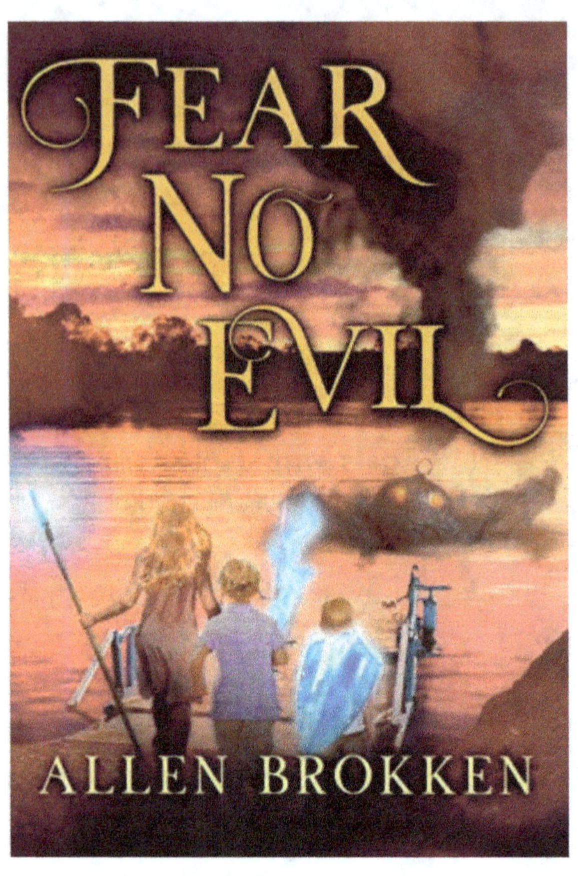

Across the land of Zoura, people and creatures alike continue to fall prey to the persuasion of darkness. The seeds of evil pollute not only those outside the Light, but those within it. Pitting neighbor against neighbor. Brother against brother. The Dark One gains ground in his pursuit to shroud the Heathlands in eternal darkness. Zoura's only hope lies with three children.

Twelve-year-old Lauren and her younger brothers, Aiden and Ethan, are determined to reignite the Tower of Light in Blooming Glen. But an attack by dark forces separates them, driving them into a valley of darkness.

Without each other or their knight protector, the three siblings must navigate the wilderness while fending off creatures tainted by evil. They fight not just for Zoura, but for their own survival.

Will the darkness overtake Lauren, Aiden, and Ethan? Or will they prove their faith 1s stronger and that they fear no evil?

Fans of *Little House on the Prairie* will feel at home in the series' classic farmstead setting. The sincerity of the children's love for one another and their desire to do the right thing will bring a smile to readers and listeners of all ages.

TEACHER GUIDE

EDUCATIONAL GOALS

The *Fear No Evil Unit Study* was developed for the third book in the Towers of Light series, a Christian fantasy adventure for middle-grade readers. It combines Biblical values and educational activities in four weeks of supplemental curriculum.

Story passages, chapter assignments, activities, and thoughtful questions foster Biblical discussion while exercising reading comprehension and critical thinking skills. Vocabulary exercises and puzzles expand students' vocabulary and provide an opportunity for students to use their reference skills while also exercising their critical thinking skills. Memory verse copy work helps students learn scripture as they practice their handwriting, and coloring sheets offer a fun opportunity for creative expression.

SUGGESTED PACING

This unit study is designed to be completed within four weeks. Each week includes around sixty pages of story content, which can be read aloud or independently. Students are encouraged to keep a reading journal for their memory verse copy work, vocabulary exercises, and to record their answers to the reading questions.

DAYS ONE THROUGH FOUR

- In their reading journal, have students copy the MEMORY VERSE and complete the VOCABULARY EXERCISE.
- Complete the DAILY READING assignment, aloud or independently.
- Read the STORY PASSAGE aloud and discuss the connection question as a group.
- Have students record their answers to the PASSAGE QUESTIONS in their journal. Answers may also be discussed as a group.

DAY FIVE

- Complete the DAILY READING assignment, aloud or independently.
- Have students recite the MEMORY VERSE.
- Use the COLORING PAGE, PUZZLE, and ACTIVITY as a fun way to wrap up the week.

TOWERS OF LIGHT

WEEK ONE
SEPARATED

Memory Verse:
"Yea, though I walk through the valley of the shadow of
death, I will fear no evil: for thou [art] with me; thy rod and
thy staff they comfort me."
— Psalms 23:4 KJV

AIDEN

VOCABULARY

WORD LIST

As part of your daily work this week, you'll need to use a dictionary and a thesaurus to look up definitions, synonyms, and antonyms for the words below.

ABOMINATION   CLAMBERED   RUDDER
BANISHED   RITE   SPYGLASS

SECRET MESSAGE

This week's vocabulary words have been used to form the message below, but it's been encrypted to keep it a secret. Determine which letter in the alphabet corresponds to each number to decode the message.

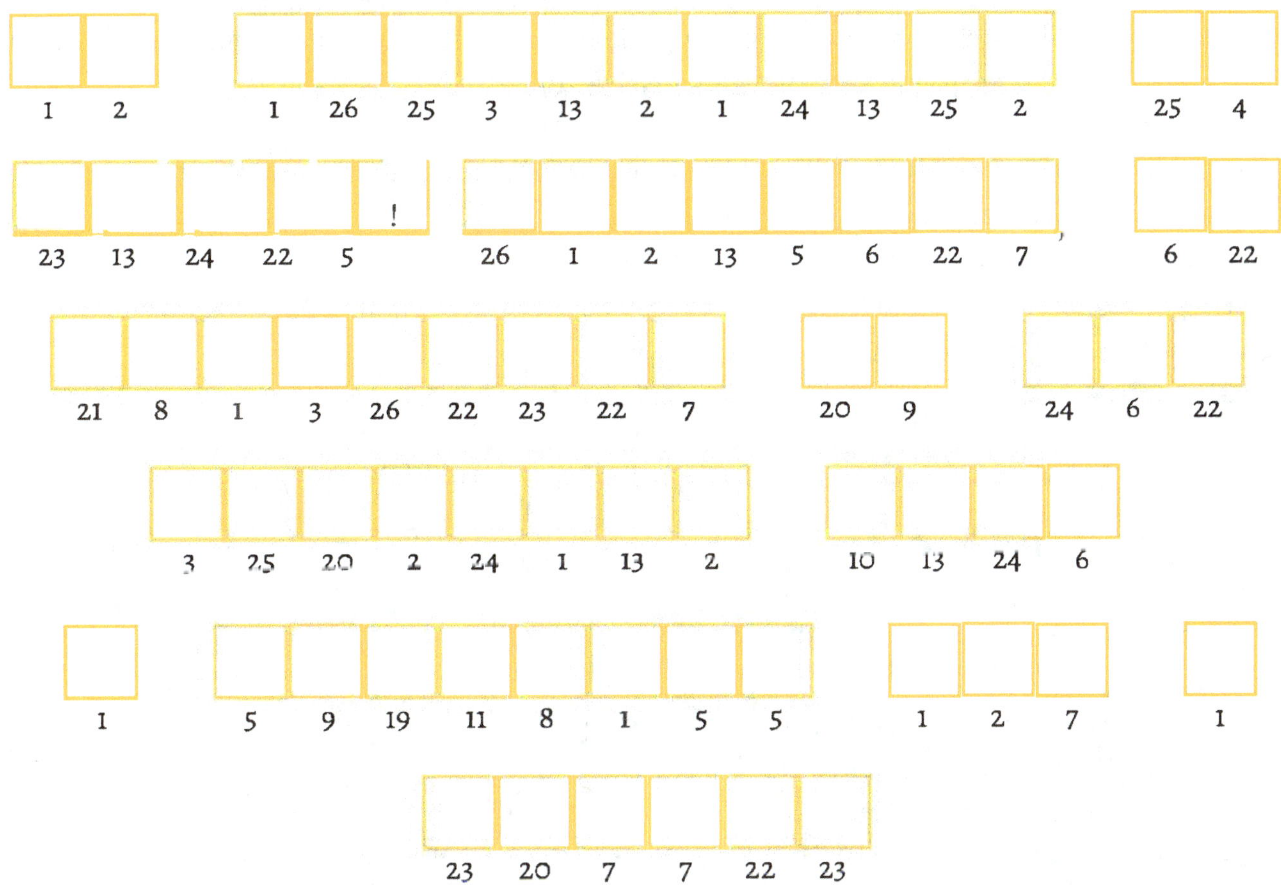

DAY ONE

MEMORY VERSE, VOCABULARY & READING

In your reading journal, copy this week's memory verse and vocabulary definitions. Then, read chapters one and two in the book.

STORY PASSAGE

Lauren's voice was strong as she read. "The Lord is my shepherd; I shall not want. He maketh me to lie down in green pastures: he leadeth me beside the still waters. He restoreth my soul: he leadeth me in the paths of righteousness for his name's sake. Yea, though I walk through the valley of the shadow of death, I will fear no evil."

A yell from outside interrupted Lauren's reading. "GIANT!"

The peace Aiden found evaporated as his heart leapt into his throat. "Oh, no! He found us!"

Aiden scrambled out of his chair, pulling his doffed sword belt along with him. *If that's the same Giant, then he defeated Uncle at the bridge.* Aiden choked back his sorrow and focused on buckling his sword belt.

Lauren and Ethan began to follow Aiden's example, but Knight Protector's strong voice halted them, "Wait children! What did that verse just say?"

Aiden paused and his brow crinkled. "Fear no evil?"

"That's right, children. The good Lord has delivered you from the valley of the shadow to our care.

WHAT FEARS DO YOU PRAY ABOUT?

PASSAGE QUESTIONS

Read the STORY PASSAGE and answer the following questions in your reading journal.

1. What does the verse that Lauren is reading mean by "The Lord is my shepherd?"
2. Did Aiden's heart really "leap into his throat?" What does that saying mean?
3. What is Uncle trying to say to the children in the last sentence of the story passage?

Joke of the Day

When does it rain money?
When there is change in the weather!

DAY TWO

MEMORY VERSE, VOCABULARY & READING

In your reading journal, copy this week's memory verse and list three synonyms for each vocabulary word. Then, read chapter three in the book.

STORY PASSAGE

"Lauren! I'm going to get Aiden." Knight Protector's voice rang from the opposite side of the wagon over the din of flopping fish and yells. "Get rope from the wagon."

Her resolved faltered, and she laid there blankly staring under the wagon at Knight Protectors boots. She was drained, like she'd been running a race for days. "I… I can't," Lauren feebly replied.

The sound of clanking metal on the other side of the wagon drowned out her voice. Knight Protector's chest piece hit the floor, and his feet appeared to leap up and out of view. She heard a big splash and assumed the old warrior was going after Aiden.

Lauren lay there for what seemed an eternity. Yells and splashing filling the night. She knew every minute counted to save Aiden, but her limbs were frozen in place.

"Lauren, I have him." Knight Protector's voice was muted, but she could hear a hint of desperation.

God, I just can't do this. The carp are going to knock me in the water too. Please help.

TELL ABOUT A TIME WHEN YOU WERE SCARED AND FELT "FROZEN."

PASSAGE QUESTIONS

Read the STORY PASSAGE and answer the following questions in your reading journal.

1. What does Lauren's "resolve faltered" mean?
2. Give some examples of how Lauren is feeling in the moment.
3. What is Lauren afraid of in this moment?

Joke of the Day

Why were the students' grades underwater?
They were all below C level!

DAY THREE

MEMORY VERSE, VOCABULARY & READING

In your reading journal, copy this week's memory verse and list three antonyms for each vocabulary word. Then, read chapters four and five in the book.

STORY PASSAGE

"A warden using the evil of the Iron Hills against the creatures we are sworn to protect! Unthinkable!" Tye's eyes narrowed. "La'Ren of the Tower, if I had not seen the Arcoirisana bless you, I would think you a liar."

Heat rushed to Lauren's cheeks. Before she could respond in her own defense, Sparkle Frog let out a croak.

Tye bowed in the direction of the Frog, "But I did see it, and can't think why you might choose to lie to me," she put an open hand out to Lauren. "Come, let us get you warm and dry. You can tell me your wild tale, and I can think about what to do about this abomination you speak of."

The heat drained from Lauren's cheeks, and a dull ache for her lost siblings overtook her. "OK, but I need you to promise me you'll help me look for my brothers."

HOW DOES IT FEEL WHEN SOMEONE DOUBTS YOU?

PASSAGE QUESTIONS

Read the STORY PASSAGE and answer the following questions in your reading journal.

1. Why did heat rush to Lauren's cheeks?
2. Why did Tye believe Lauren's story?
3. Why did Tye use the word abomination?
4. What does Lauren ask Tye to help her do?

Joke of the Day

Why did the baker's credit card get declined?
He didn't have enough dough!

DAY FOUR

MEMORY VERSE, VOCABULARY & READING

In your reading journal, copy this week's memory verse and draw a picture definition for each vocabulary word. Then, read chapter six in the book.

STORY PASSAGE

Behind the attacker, a group of a dozen similarly tattered Bjorn-born stood blocking the exit from what used to be the back of the ferry. "Aiden! Sissy! Help! I'm surrounded!" Ethan's yell caused all of the Bjorn-born to flinch back and look all around. When help didn't come, they moved in closer, menacing Ethan with their spears.

He looked for his shield and remembered dropping it in the wagon just before the lights went out. He was alone and unarmed. Seeking divine inspiration, he looked up and realized the sky above them had the Darkness haze they saw over the parson's house. A chill went down his spine and weakened his knees.

What did the Good Book say? In the valley of the shadow, fear no evil. God had helped him defeat the hell hounds and save Tok's bear; God would save him now too. He took a deep breath, and confidence filled his chest. These guys were littler than he was by at least a head. If he could get past them, he could outrun them. Maybe if he talked to them, he could squeeze past.

HOW DOES GOD HELP GIVE YOU CONFIDENCE?

PASSAGE QUESTIONS

Read the STORY PASSAGE and answer the following questions in your reading journal.

1. What does it mean when it says the Bjorn-born were "menacing Ethan with their spears?"
2. Why did a chill go down Ethan's spine that "weakened his knees?"
3. How did Ethan regain his confidence?
4. What was Ethan's idea?

Joke of the Day

Why was everyone grouchy after drinking the apple cider?
It was made from crab apples!

DAY FIVE

READING & MEMORY VERSE

Read chapter seven in the book. Then, recite this week's memory verse aloud and complete the activity below. Include the coloring page and vocabulary puzzle with today's activities.

ACTIVITY: RUDDER EXPERIMENT

MATERIALS

- Lid to a small, square, plastic container
- Small dowel rod
- Rubber band
- Large popsicle stick
- Box cutter (to be used by adult)

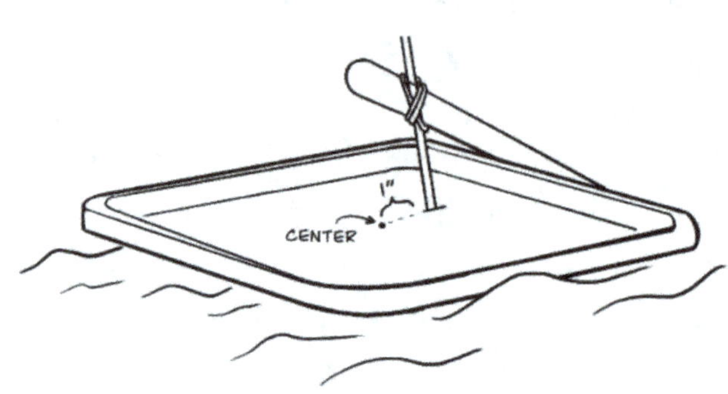

INSTRUCTIONS

An adult needs to use a box cutter to make a hole in the lid. The lid will be your raft. Make the hole about an inch away from the center, towards one of the sides. It needs to be big enough for the rod to turn, but still fit snugly so the rod doesn't fall through. Cut the dowel rod in half. Attach the popsicle stick flat against the rod with a rubber band, and pointed down at about a 45-degree angle. Then insert your rod into the hole in the lid. Now, you have a raft!

Place the raft into the water with the dowel rod up. The popsicle stick should stick into the water enough to use as a rudder. If not, adjust the rubber band and popsicle stick to get a better angle. You should be able to turn your dowel rod different ways to adjust the rudder and change the direction your raft floats.

HOW DO YOU USE GOD'S WORD TO HELP YOU STEER IN THE WORLD?

WEEK TWO
ALLIANCES

Memory Verse:
"Fear thou not; for I am with thee: be not dismayed; for I am thy God: I will strengthen thee; yea, I will help thee; yea, I will uphold thee with the right hand of my righteousness."
— Isaiah 41:10 KJV

LAUREN

VOCABULARY

WORD LIST

As part of your daily work this week, you'll need to use a dictionary and a thesaurus to look up definitions, synonyms, and antonyms for the words below.

CHARRED   GRANDEUR   RAMSHACKLE
FORAGING   FALTERED   VENGEANCE

WORD SCRAMBLE

Rearrange each group of letters below to unscramble the words.

DRAECHR

__ __ __ __ __ __ __

NAIGGOFR

__ __ __ __ __ __ __ __

ARERDGNU

__ __ __ __ __ __ __ __

ETFAELRD

__ __ __ __ __ __ __ __

CKLASMREHA

__ __ __ __ __ __ __ __ __ __

VNNEGACEE

__ __ __ __ __ __ __ __ __

DAY ONE

MEMORY VERSE, VOCABULARY & READING

In your reading journal, copy this week's memory verse and vocabulary definitions. Then, read chapter eight in the book.

STORY PASSAGE

"But my ma'ma tells me that is not our way, that we must save this creature because it knows not what it does."

"I think your mother is right," Lauren said. "After I knocked the Darkness out of Tok's bear, it let Tok get on its back and ride as if they were best of friends."

Tye put a hand on Lauren's shoulder. "La'Ren of the Tower, do you think your spear can save this bear?"

God, is this why you brought me here? A wave of power coursed through Lauren as she reached for her spear. It immediately came to life.

Tye gaped at the sight. "La'Ren of the Tower, I did not believe you. But this is true power."

"It's not my power; God gives it to me when he wants." Lauren continued, "Saving this bear must be part of his plan."

"Come. The bear will be foraging now. We should eat." Tye walked towards the fire. "Tell me more about your God while I prepare the meal."

Lauren was suddenly overwhelmed. *God how can I explain the whole Good Book over lunch?*

HAS TELLING OTHERS ABOUT GOD EVER OVERWHELMED YOU?

PASSAGE QUESTIONS

Read the STORY PASSAGE and answer the following questions in your reading journal.

1. What does Tye's ma'ma mean when she says the bear "knows not what it does?"
2. What experience does Lauren have to give to Tye that her mother is right?
3. Explain what overwhelmed means?
4. Why does Lauren feel so overwhelmed?

> **Joke of the Day**
>
> There's one good thing about being hit in the head with a bottle of soda. It's a soft drink!

DAY TWO

MEMORY VERSE, VOCABULARY & READING

In your reading journal, copy this week's memory verse and list three synonyms for each vocabulary word. Then, read chapter nine in the book.

STORY PASSAGE

Ethan could smell the stuff in the gourd now, and it stunk. Like when cider went bad. He definitely didn't want that. The meat reminded him of the time Father burned a rotten coon on the trash pile.

Not knowing exactly how to respond, he just said, "No, thank you."

"You eat meat, drink kefir." The warrior shook the items at him

"My Daddy wouldn't like that," Ethan pulled out a tomato from his pouch. "I have food."

"Bah! Ba'bee food!" the warrior spat and glared at Ethan. "Long trip to hoo'man camp. Need real food."

"Well, I guess I'm a baby then," spilled out of Ethan's mouth before he could think about it. *What did I just do?* His stomach clenched. *Will he make me eat their poison food?*

"Bah!" The warrior shook his head then took another drink of the awful stuff in the gourd. "Ba'bee, stay here." He pointed at a six-foot log lying on the ground.

Ethan obeyed without a word, thankful for not being forced to eat the Darkness food.

HOW CAN GOD HELP US STAND UP TO OTHERS?

PASSAGE QUESTIONS

Read the STORY PASSAGE and answer the following questions in your reading journal.

1. What is making the food bad?
2. List the ways that Ethan responds to Chief's pressure to eat the awful food.
3. Why does Chief think Ethan needs to eat the food?

Joke of the Day

What did the first sock say to the second one in the dryer?
I'll see you next time around!

DAY THREE

MEMORY VERSE, VOCABULARY & READING

In your reading journal, copy this week's memory verse and list three antonyms for each vocabulary word. Then, read chapters ten and eleven in the book.

STORY PASSAGE

"This savior, he takes your disobedience against your Elders away?" Tye was crying now.

"Yeah, that's one thing." Deep down, Lauren was still feeling guilty for just lying on the ferry's floor when Knight Protector needed help, "During the battle, my elder asked me to throw a rope."

Lauren faltered a moment as her tears began. "I was too afraid of the fish that were attacking us, and I hid instead. Knight Protector and my brother Aiden were both stunned by the giant catfish because I didn't help when I was asked."

Lauren broke down, and Tye moved to her side and put an arm around her. "I too disobeyed my elder. I was tasked to watch my brother. Instead, I left him sleeping on his own while I went to the creek for a swim. When I returned, the bear had him and was taking him into the woods. By the time I got weapons to chase her, she was gone."

They both cried over their failures to save their brothers. "The Good Book says if we believe in the Savior and confess our misdeeds, we will be forgiven."

WHAT DOES THE BIBLE SAY ABOUT FORGIVENESS?

PASSAGE QUESTIONS

Read the STORY PASSAGE and answer the following questions in your reading journal.

1. What did Lauren feel guilty about in the story passage?
2. What happened to Tye's brother?
3. What knowledge did Lauren have that reassured them?

Joke of the Day

What does Meow Meow like to eat on his birthday?
Cake and mice cream!

DAY FOUR

MEMORY VERSE, VOCABULARY & READING

In your reading journal, copy this week's memory verse and draw a picture definition for each vocabulary word. Then, read chapter twelve in the book.

STORY PASSAGE

If he was going to be the leader of the Iron Hills, he needed to take charge now. He held out the chalice in one hand and poured it back into the pool. "By my own hands, I defeated Ursa and reclaimed the Horn of Power from the outsider's temple; it will be by my own hands that I take the waters of my destiny."

The guards on either side of the pool immediately snapped their spears to his neck. The high priestess lazily held up her hand. "Hold." She sighed. "What is this, blasphemy?"

"Your Holiness, only a truly penitent man can hope to lead the people of the hills." He gingerly avoided the spears at his neck as he slowly knelt in front of the pool. Then he looked up at her. "To stand imperiously over the people as the waters make their choice would surely condemn me to dust."

The high priestess' demeanor cracked. At first her eyes went wide, then she recoiled slightly. *Gotcha.* She knew that if he drank from the pool and didn't die that her days as ruler were over. He also knew, with such a pious answer, she'd have a revolt if she didn't let him finish his way.

HOW CAN YOU TELL IF SOMEONE IS GOOD OR JUST LOOKS THAT WAY?

PASSAGE QUESTIONS

Read the STORY PASSAGE and answer the following questions in your reading journal.

1. Why won't Refi'Cul's evil plan work if he has to drink from a cup?
2. How does he trick the high priestess into letting him drink from the pool with his hands?
3. What is a penitent man?

Joke of the Day

I heard a joke about a chocolate bar, and it wasn't very funny.
So, I just snickered!

DAY FIVE

READING & MEMORY VERSE

Read chapter thirteen in the book. Then, recite this week's memory verse aloud and complete the activity below. Include the coloring page and vocabulary puzzle with today's activities.

ACTIVITY: ORANGE SURGERY

MATERIALS

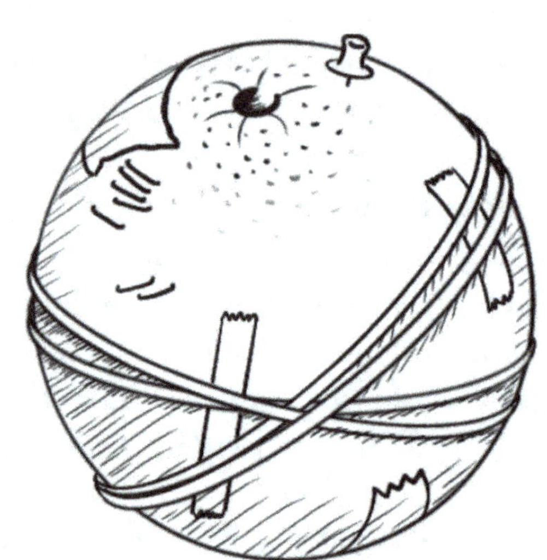

- An orange and a paper plate for each person
- An assortment of office supplies (various kinds of tape, staplers, paper clips, rubber bands, strings, glue, and anything else that might help put an orange back together)
- A timer
- Wet wipes or paper towels for cleanup

INSTRUCTIONS

Set a timer for two minutes. During which, each person will peel their oranges and pull apart the slices. Place the peels and slices in two separate piles on the plates. Then try completing the reconstruction challenge. Gather the office supplies together, placing where everyone participating can reach them, and set a timer for five minutes. Use the office supplies to put your orange back together before time runs out.

OFFICE SUPPLIES CAN ONLY BE USED ONE AT A TIME. If you are using the tape, you must return the tape before you can use another item, like the stapler. The person whose orange looks the most like it originally did at the end of five minutes wins. Pick someone not doing the challenge to be the judge.

HOW ARE THE EFFECTS OF SIN SIMILAR TO THE ORANGE? WHO CAN UNDO THE EFFECTS OF SIN IN OUR LIVES? HOW DOES HE DO THAT?

WEEK THREE
TRAPPED

Memory Verse:
"For God hath not given us the spirit of fear; but of power,
and of love, and of a sound mind."
— 2 Timothy 1:7 KJV

ETHAN

VOCABULARY

WORD LIST

As part of your daily work this week, you'll need to use a dictionary and a thesaurus to look up definitions, synonyms, and antonyms for the words below.

APOTHECARY	LEAN-TO	STALACTITES
INFIRMARY	OMINOUS	TUNIC

MAZE

Help the kids find their way! Trace a path from the center of the maze to the outside.

DAY ONE

MEMORY VERSE, VOCABULARY & READING

In your reading journal, copy this week's memory verse and vocabulary definitions. Then, read chapters fourteen and fifteen in the book.

STORY PASSAGE

"Hoo'man, why bear not eat you?" the creature asked as Ethan walked to Baby Bear.

"Because I shared my food with him." Ethan patted his pouch. "He likes carrots."

"Yes, yes. Share with the bear." Besta sat down on the ledge. "Before Darkness, that was way."

Baby Bear nudged the apple in Ethan's hand. He gave it to his friend but hoped it wouldn't make him sick.

"Now bears get dark." Besta hung her head. "Now bears just eat meat. Eat my babies." Ethan couldn't see in the dim flickering light, but he thought she was crying. *She must be a grandma Bjorn-born like I thought.* He frowned, and his eyes got a little watery, too.

"Chief think. Eat meat. Grow strong. Defeat bear." Besta shook her head. "That not our way."

He felt really bad for all of the good Bjorn-born. They didn't have a tower to protect them from the Darkness. Now he understood why Father wanted them to light the tower in Blooming Glen. These people needed the Light.

DO YOU KNOW OF PEOPLE THAT NEED GOD'S LIGHT?

PASSAGE QUESTIONS

Read the STORY PASSAGE and answer the following questions in your reading journal.

1. What was Ethan's answer when Besta asked him why the bear didn't eat him?
2. What did Besta say happened "before Darkness?"
3. Why was Besta sad?
4. What helped Ethan understand why they needed to light the tower in Blooming Glen?

DAY TWO

MEMORY VERSE, VOCABULARY & READING

In your reading journal, copy this week's memory verse and list three synonyms for each vocabulary word. Then, read chapter sixteen in the book.

STORY PASSAGE

"You think the Darkness can stand against that?" Mother pointed to Aiden's sword.

First Sister faltered for a moment. "They took all our weapons, control hell hounds, and have blocked the light in the temple. I've seen the power your son wields, but is he alone enough?"

Mother looked at Aiden. "What do you think?"

Aiden stood there for a moment, concentrating on his breathing to clear his mind. *God, I don't know what to do. I want to save Father, but is that what we need to do now?* The fire on the sword went out. Aiden felt the chill of the mountains and knew the right thing to do.

He swallowed a lump in his throat. "Mama, I don't fear the evil. But I don't think that's our mission. We need to shine our light in Blooming Glen, and then save Daddy." As if to emphasize the point, the sword erupted into flame.

Mother nodded as a tear rolled down her cheek.

WHAT DO YOU DO WHEN YOU ARE FACED WITH A DIFFICULT CHOICE?

PASSAGE QUESTIONS

Read the STORY PASSAGE and answer the following questions in your reading journal.

1. How did Aiden make his decision?
2. What made his choice clear?
3. How did Mama feel about Aiden's choice?

Joke of the Day

Why does the NBA require basketball players to wear bibs at dinner?
Because they're dribblers!

DAY THREE

MEMORY VERSE, VOCABULARY & READING

In your reading journal, copy this week's memory verse and list three antonyms for each vocabulary word. Then, read chapters seventeen and eighteen in the book.

STORY PASSAGE

Ethan caught the glint of green again and then gingerly reached in to grab it. He pulled carefully and found a green jewel in his fingers attached to the hilt of a long dagger. In Ethan's small hands, it was almost a short sword. An oilcloth fell to the ground as he pulled the blade free.

Ethan's heart raced that he could break the lock on Baby Bear's cage. The light refracting through the jewel dazzled him, but the blood rolling off the back of his hand brought him back to the imminent danger around them.

He put the dagger down for a second and wrapped the oilcloth around his wounded hand, then he picked the dagger up in his right hand and the food bag in his left.

Lok looked Ethan in the eye, "We go!" the roar of the bear punctuated his urgency.

"Yes, let's go." They hurried out of the barge. Ethan was surprised to see a pile of carrots just outside the main glow of the fire. So, he stopped. "I can add a few more."

"No, food for bear," Lok grabbed Ethan's arm and pulled him. "E'tan, go fast."

HAS GOD EVER GIVEN HELP TO YOU AT JUST THE RIGHT MOMENT?

PASSAGE QUESTIONS

Read the STORY PASSAGE and answer the following questions in your reading journal.

1. What did Ethan find in the box? What did he think it would help him do?
2. Do you think the oil cloth fell out of the box by coincidence?
3. Why do you think Lok insisted on leaving the carrots for the mama bear?

DAY FOUR

MEMORY VERSE, VOCABULARY & READING

In your reading journal, copy this week's memory verse and draw a picture definition for each vocabulary word. Then, read chapter ninteen in the book.

STORY PASSAGE

"Tye! You have the Light!" Lauren cried in triumph as she finally moved the boy to face that direction. "Strike the bear now!"

The bear turned towards them, and Tye threw the spear with all she had. The holy blade struck true in the bear's chest, and a pulse of blue-green light cascaded out from that point to cover the bear in a flash of light. It flopped unconscious to the ground.

The shield's light dimmed considerably but still provided some light to the clearing. Lauren helped Tye's brother off the ground and pointed him towards the giantess.

Thunder boomed, and rain began to fall. "Tye, we should get in out of the rain. The bear won't wake up for a while, but it should be friendly now."

Tye merely nodded and scooped her brother up in her arms. She laughed as tears of joy ran down her face. "La'Ren of the Tower, you saved my brother! I can return to my people redeemed!"

Lauren shook her head, "No, Tye. You have the power of God's Light in you. The Savior redeemed you." Lauren followed the joyful siblings into the cave.

**DO YOU KNOW OF A TIME WHEN THE SAVIOR
CHANGED SOMEONE'S LIFE?**

PASSAGE QUESTIONS

Read the STORY PASSAGE and answer the following questions in your reading journal.

1. What happened to the bear as it turned to attack?
2. Why did Tye think Lauren saved her brother?
3. What sentence describes the emotion Tye felt when her brother was saved?

Joke of the Day

What kind of shoes do Ninjas like best?

Sneakers!

DAY FIVE

READING & MEMORY VERSE

Read chapter twenty in the book. Then, recite this week's memory verse aloud and complete the activity below. Include the coloring page and vocabulary puzzle with today's activities.

ACTIVITY: MAKE A CAVE

MATERIALS

- Playdough
- A small glass bowl
- Sugar cubes
- Warm water
- A toothpick

INSTRUCTIONS

Place a thick layer of playdough in the bottom of the bowl. Next, put sugar cubes on top of the playdough, and add a second, thin layer of playdough on top. Flatten the top layer of playdough over the sugar cubes like a roof, but don't squish it down into the cubes. Make sure the playdough roof edges are pushed against the edges of the bowl.

Poke some holes through the top layer of playdough with a toothpick, and pour water into the bowl to make it "rain." The sugar cubes will melt, leaving a cave!

The sugar cubes and playdough represent a layer of limestone rock between two layers of earth. Over a long period of time, rainwater eats away the limestone layers of rock in the earth, leaving a hollow space.

SIMILARLY, JESUS OFFERS SALVATION TO WASH AWAY OUR SINS. WHAT CAN WE DO TO FILL THE SPACE IN OUR LIVES WITH GOD'S LOVE?

WEEK FOUR
RESCUED

Memory Verse:
"I sought the LORD, and he heard me, and delivered me from all my fears."
— Psalms 34:4

VOCABULARY

WORD LIST

As part of your daily work this week, you'll need to use a dictionary and a thesaurus to look up definitions, synonyms, and antonyms for the words below.

ANGUISH	FACETS	OVERSHADOWED
CONSOLED	HILT	PENDULUM

WORD SEARCH

Find and circle the hidden vocabulary words in the puzzle below. Words may appear up, down, forwards, backwards, or diagonally.

ABOMINATION	CONSOLED	INFIRMARY	RITE
ANGUISH	FACETS	LEAN-TO	RUDDER
APOTHECARY	FALTERED	OMINOUS	SPYGLASS
BANISHED	FORAGING	OVERSHADOWED	STALACTITES
CHARRED	GRANDEUR	PENDULUM	TUNIC
CLAMBERED	HILT	RAMSHACKLE	VENGEANCE

```
Q K M L F A C E T S L I W G Y M W C V Q U Z V M P
A Q E M F E B K M U U D L N Z A R R L K B H Q A N
X V F J J Y I O D T R W M H P J D R R U D D E R Y
O S R G R J T J M L U A I A N G U I S H R K A D K
S V Q F R F T F E I V N M O R Q R T E C C Q R D D
I L E Z C A F W A H N E I S C X V E V Z G P H N O
N B P R S L N O H L D A N C H A P O T H E C A R Y
F A E C S P A D R L T M T G Y A G X L E A N T O D
I N N T P H Y M E A K E M I E J C C O N S O L E D
R I D P X A A G B U G J R I O A M K C H A R R E D
M S U F T K T D L E R I L E U N N T L H I L T C M
A H L P H Z T N O A R K N A D O Y C G E Z X D Z K
R E U X P U Z W A W S E N G I V U B E X J S K Z S
Y D M M B Z J T K K E S D A I J O F J J N I K S G
S T A L A C T I T E S D E S A A K O M I N O U S W
```

DAY ONE

MEMORY VERSE, VOCABULARY & READING

In your reading journal, copy this week's memory verse and vocabulary definitions. Then, read chapters twenty-one and twenty-two in the book.

STORY PASSAGE

Ethan's heart leapt, and tears burst from his eyes at the familiar voice. "Sissy, I need you! Help me!"

Through his tear-filled eyes, he made out Lauren rushing forward with his shield on her arm as the bear dropped to all fours and revealed the largest woman he had ever seen behind it, holding Lauren's spear.

"No! bear eat ba'bee hoo'man!" Chief yelled as he rushed between Ethan and the bear to block the rescuers' advance. "We eat bear. Get strong."

The Bjorn-born that had faded into the trees re-appeared spears in hand.

"That is not our way," Lok called out

The Bjorn-born encircling them seemed to falter.

"Get them!" Chief threw his spear at the bear.

Lauren blocked the shot with the shield, as the giant returned fire with the spear. It caught Chief in the forehead and catapulted him to the ground behind Ethan. *That giant is powerful!*

LAUREN AND ETHAN WERE SO HAPPY TO SEE EACH OTHER! SAY A PRAYER FOR SOMEONE THAT YOU WISH YOU COULD SEE TODAY.

PASSAGE QUESTIONS

Read the STORY PASSAGE and answer the following questions in your reading journal.

1. Why did Chief want the bear to eat Ethan?
2. What words described how Ethan felt when he realized that Lauren was there?
3. Did the Bjorn-born help Chief?
4. Why did Ethan think Tye was so powerful?

DAY TWO

MEMORY VERSE, VOCABULARY & READING

In your reading journal, copy this week's memory verse and list three synonyms for each vocabulary word. Then, read chapters twenty-three and twenty-four in the book.

STORY PASSAGE

The lock and the iron around the door looked very corroded. Aiden sliced it, but this time Mother was unable to open the door. The hinges were rusted shut.

"Could we get some help?" Mother called.

"I can get it." Aiden grunted through gritted teeth as he hobbled to the other side of the door.

"Aiden, wait!" Mother rushed to his side.

He whacked the hinges, and the door slammed down, cutting off the light at the bottom. It began to tip inward toward them.

Mother tackled Aiden with a shoulder charge, his sword flung away, and it's light extinguished as it flew. They landed on the dusty floor as the door slammed behind them.

Daddy Duck flew into the warehouse and landed next to Aiden, poking Aiden's head with his bill.

"I'm OK, Daddy Duck," Aiden whispered.

First Sister spoke up, "Sisters make haste. The enemy must be alerted to our escape route."

HAVE YOU EVER BEEN TOO IMPATIENT TO STOP AND LISTEN?

PASSAGE QUESTIONS

Read the STORY PASSAGE and answer the following questions in your reading journal.

1. Why do you think Mother told Aiden to wait?
2. Why do you think Aiden didn't listen?
3. Name three things that happened because Aiden did not listen.

Joke of the Day

I picked some apples the other day
that I think are time travelers.
They're full of wormholes!

DAY THREE

MEMORY VERSE, VOCABULARY & READING

In your reading journal, copy this week's memory verse and list three antonyms for each vocabulary word. Then, read chapter twenty-five in the book.

STORY PASSAGE

Skull Crusher put the net with Ethan down—more gently than before—and opened the net all the way. Ethan had the water jug wrapped to his chest. Tye where are you?

"Get in the net!" Skull Crusher barked. Seeing how Ethan was sitting gave Lauren an idea, so she turned her belt, so the pouch with the vegetables and hidden dagger was to her front.

"What's in the bag?" Skull Crusher demanded.

Lauren reached in and pulled out a piece of carrot. "Food. Do you want to wait until we've had a full lunch, or do you want to get going?" Deep down she hoped he'd take the full lunch option.

"Sit down, before I knock you down." He demanded.

A sideways smile cracked her lips, knowing her taunting worked. He let her keep the pouch with the dagger in it. If Tye didn't come soon, she had a backup plan.

Then she sat down on the net beside Ethan with her arms wrapped around her knees. She bent over and took a sip of water from the jug Ethan was holding.

Without a word, Skull Crusher pulled the net tight and slung them over his back.

HAVE YOU EVER HAD TO DEAL WITH A BULLY?

PASSAGE QUESTIONS

Read the STORY PASSAGE and answer the following questions in your reading journal.

1. How did Lauren distract Skull Crusher from looking in her pouch?
2. Why didn't Lauren want Skull Crusher looking in her pouch?
3. Why did Lauren hope that Skull Crusher would take "the full lunch option?"
4. What do you think Lauren's backup plan was?

DAY FOUR

MEMORY VERSE, VOCABULARY & READING

In your reading journal, copy this week's memory verse and draw a picture definition for each vocabulary word. Then, read chapter twenty-six in the book.

STORY PASSAGE

Mother stood. "Now we need to get out of here. What about the horses?"

Knight Protector shook his head. "There's no time to saddle them. We're just as likely to have a fall as get away cleanly."

Uncle nodded. "What're you thinkin', you old fool."

"Heath Warden, can you hide this family in the forest while I draw the enemy away?" Knight Protector started putting bit and bridle on the horses in their stalls.

"Yes! We can escape to a safe place." The giantess put her sling over her shoulder.

"I just pulled yer ragged hide out of the river. Don't go off and get yerself killed," Uncle said as he patted the old man on the shoulder.

"Go with your family and get them to Blooming Glen. All depends on it." Knight Protector shook his hand.

The kids rushed up and gave him a hug.

"Thanks for getting us this far. Mama and Uncle will get us the rest of the way." Lauren offered.

"Yes, they will, and God willing, I'll meet you there."

PASSAGE QUESTIONS

Read the STORY PASSAGE and answer the following questions in your reading journal.

1. Who are they trying to get away from?
2. What has just taken place?
3. What is Knight Protector going to do with all of the horses?
4. Why does everything depend on the family getting to Blooming Glen?

Joke of the Day

What book did Lauren get from the library for Meow Meow?
The Prince and the PAW-PURR!

DAY FIVE

READING & MEMORY VERSE

Read the epilogue in the book. Then, recite this week's memory verse aloud and complete the activity below. Include the coloring page and vocabulary puzzle with today's activities.

ACTIVITY: SALAMANDER SLIME

MATERIALS

- Elmer's white school glue, 8 oz.
- Contact saline solution, 1 1/2 Tbsp. (or more as needed)
- Baking soda, 1 Tbsp.
- Food coloring (optional)

INSTRUCTIONS

Squeeze the bottle of glue into a bowl. Add food coloring, if desired. Mix in baking soda and blend together well. (Make sure to add the food coloring before adding the contact solution!) Next, stir in the contact solution and knead until it holds together well.

If the mixture is too sticky, add more contac solution — ½ Tbsp. at a time. The contact solution changes the consistency of the mixture: more makes it thicker and less keeps it slimier.

A mat or plastic tablecloth is recommended for playing with the slime. Be careful to keep it away from hair! Recipe makes about one cup of slime.

HOW DOES LISTENING TO YOUR PARENTS AND TO GOD'S WORD KEEP YOU OUT OF STICKY SITUATIONS?

ANSWER KEY

WEEK ONE: SEPARATED

DAY ONE

1. The Lord is our shepherd because he cares for us, protects us, and laid His life down to save us. We should learn to know his voice and follow Him.
2. No, his heart didn't actually move. It means that he felt suddenly frightened.
3. Uncle is trying to reassure the children to have faith that God would protect them. He is reminding them that God delivered them there, where there were many people that were willing to fight for the children.

DAY TWO

1. It means that Lauren lost her courage for a moment. She was too scared to do what was asked of her.
2. It says she was "blankly staring," "she was drained," and "her limbs were frozen."
3. She is scared because Aiden was knocked in the water. She is scared of the carp knocking her into the water too.

DAY THREE

1. She thinks that Tye is calling her a liar.
2. She believed Lauren because she said that she saw the Arcoirisana bless her.
3. Abomination means something that causes hatred or a feeling of disgust or loathing. Tye cannot imagine another warden using evil against creatures that they have always been sworn to protect.
4. She asks Tye to help her find her brothers.

DAY FOUR

1. Menacing means to threaten. So, they were threatening Ethan with their spears.
2. He felt afraid. He realized that the Darkness was in that place.
3. Ethan thought about what the Good Book said, and how God had helped him before.
4. He thought he could distract them by talking to them and then outrun them.

SECRET MESSAGE

An abomination of rites! Banished, he clambered up the mountain with a spyglass and a rudder.

WEEK TWO: ALLIANCES

DAY ONE

1. She means that the bear doesn't really understand what it is doing because it is corrupted by the Darkness.
2. Lauren remembers that after she knocked the Darkness out of Tok's bear with her spear, it became kind again.
3. Feeling overwhelmed by something causes many strong emotions all at once that are often stressful, and it feels like you cannot overcome the situation.
4. Lauren feels overwhelmed because she knows that trying to explain salvation to Tye is very important. She wants to do it right, and she thinks that she has to explain the whole Good Book.

DAY TWO

1. The food has been cooked over the censer, therefore it has been corrupted by the Darkness.
2. Ethan tries saying things like "No, thank you," and "My Daddy wouldn't like that." He tells Chief he has his own food. When Chief calls his food "Ba'bee food," Ethan replies, "Well, I guess I'm a baby then."
3. Chief has already been corrupted by the Darkness. In his mind, he thinks that if Ethan eats the food, he will become strong like him.

DAY THREE

1. She felt guilty because she was scared of the carp and hid when they were attacked on the ferry. Without her help, Aiden and Knight Protector were stung by the carp.
2. Tye's brother was taken by a mother bear. Tye was supposed to be watching him but left him sleeping while she went for a swim in the creek.
3. Lauren told Tye about what is says in the Good Book. Lauren tells her it says, "...if we believe in the Savior and confess our misdeeds, we will be forgiven."

DAY FOUR

1. It won't work because everyone would see him crush the globe into the water. He needed to crush the globe into the actual pool of water for nobody to see him do it.
2. He uses words like "by my own hands." He says that "it will be by my own hands that I take the waters of my destiny." He claims that he is being too superior by standing over the people while the water makes its choice. By pretending to be timid and respectful, Refi'Cul is getting the high priestess to give him his way.
3. A penitent man is someone who is humble or repentant.

WEEK TWO: ALLIANCES

WORD SCRAMBLE

1. DRAECHR: Charred
2. NAIGGOFR: Foraging
3. ARERDGNU: Grandeur
4. ETFAELRD: Faltered
5. CKLASMREHA: Ramshackle
6. VNNEGACEE: Vengeance

WEEK THREE: TRAPPED

DAY ONE

1. Ethan said that it was because he "shared his food with him."
2. Besta implied that before Darkness they shared food with bears too.
3. Besta was sad because the Darkness had corrupted the bears and her people.
4. All of the things that Besta told him made Ethan realize how much they needed the Light to protect them.

DAY TWO

1. He prayed and asked God for help.
2. When he told Mama what he thought they should do, his sword erupted into flame.
3. She agreed by nodding, but she was still sad to leave Father.

DAY THREE

1. Ethan found a dagger in the box. He thought it would help him free Baby Bear.
2. Answers will vary, but consider how God sometimes puts things in just the right places at just the right times.
3. Lok's people naturally take care of the bears. However, it was also used as a strategy to help slow Mama bear down.

DAY FOUR

1. Tye threw Lauren's spear at the bear and hit it in the chest.
2. Tye thought Lauren saved her brother because she brought him out of the cave. She did not yet realize that she had the power of God's Light.
3. "She laughed as tears of joy ran down her face."

MAZE

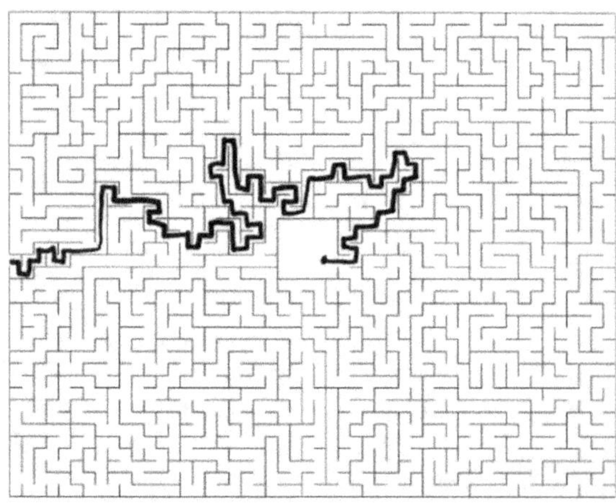

WEEK FOUR: RESCUED

DAY ONE

1. Chief believed if the bear ate Ethan that they could eat the bear and get strong.
2. His "heart leapt" and "tears burst from his eyes."
3. The other Bjorn-born with Chief came out with their spears, but they seemed to "falter" when they heard Lok say that what they were doing was not their "way."
4. Ethan thought Tye was powerful because of her size, and how Chief was "catapulted"when she hit him with Lauren's spear.

DAY TWO

1. She knew what would happen to the door if he cut through it in that spot.
2. Aiden didn't listen because he was hurt and was being impatient.
3. The door slammed and tipped inward towards them. Mother dove and tackled Aiden out of the way. The door crashed to the floor loudly, alerting the enemy to their escape route.

DAY THREE

1. Lauren told him there was food in her pouch. Knowing he was in a hurry, she asked him if he wanted to sit down and have a "full lunch."
2. She didn't want him looking in the pouch because the dagger was in it.
3. If Skull Crusher would have agreed to a "full lunch" it would have slowed them down more, giving Tye a chance to catch up to them.
4. Her backup plan was to use the dagger to cut them free from the net.

DAY FOUR

1. They are trying to get away from Refi'Cul and the Steele Brothers.
2. They have just defeated Skull Crusher in a battle. He has been hit with Lauren's spear and is unconscious.
3. Knight Protector is going to take all of the horses and lead them off in a different direction than the family, in hopes that the enemy follows him.
4. If they can get to Blooming Glen and light the tower there, then everything and everyone hit by its Light will be protected from the Darkness.

WEEK FOUR: RESCUED

WORD SEARCH

Q K M L F A C E T S L I W G Y M W C V Q U Z V M P
A Q E M F E B K M U U D L N Z A R R L K B H Q A N
X V F J J Y I O D T R W M H P J D R R U D D E R Y
O S R G R J T J M L U A I A N G U I S H R K A D K
S V Q F R F T F E I V N M O R Q R T E C C Q R D D
I L E Z C A F W A H N E I S C X V E V Z G P H N O
N B P R S L N O H L D A N C H A P O T H E C A R Y
F A E C S P A D R L T M T G Y A G X L E A N T O D
I N N T P H Y M E A K E M I E J C C O N S O L E D
R I D P X A A G B U G J R I O A M K C H A R R E D
M S U F T K T D L E R I L E U N T L H I L T C M
A H L P H Z T N O A R K N A D O Y C G E Z X D Z K
R E U X P U Z W A W S E N G I V U B E X J S K Z S
Y D M M B Z J T K K E S D A I J O F J N I K S G
S T A L A C T I T E S D E S A A K O M I N O U S W

STAND AGAINST THE DARKNESS

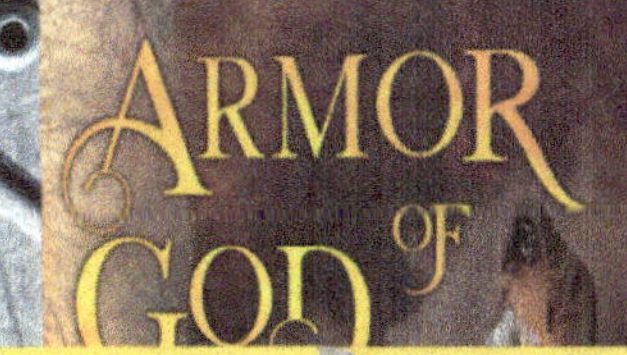

As defenders of the light, three siblings embark on a journey to stop the dark forces invading their land. An epic Christian fantasy series for middle-grade readers.

"The Tower of Light series has everything you could want in a good book series, from fantasy and adventure to good Christian values all rolled into one."

—SHAUNA VANDEPOL
THE HOMESCHOOL REVIEW CREW

TOWERS OF LIGHT
TowersofLight.net

www.ingramcontent.com/pod-product-compliance
Lightning Source LLC
Chambersburg PA
CBHW080605300726

48975CB00011B/2801